SUPER DOOPER JEZEBEL

Tony Ross

For Jan and Paul

This edition published in 2002 by Diamond Books
77-85 Fulham Palace Road
Hammersmith, London, W6 8JB

First Published in Great Britain 1988 by Andersen Press Ltd
Published in Picture Lions 1989

ISBN: 0 00 763542 7

Picture Lions is an imprint of the Children's Division,
part of the Collins Publishing Group
8 Grafton Street, London W1X 3LA

Copyright © 1988 Tony Ross

Printed by Imago

SUPER DOOPER JEZEBEL

Tony Ross

Jezebel was perfect in every way. She was so perfect
she was called Super Dooper Jezebel.

When other children came out of school, they were sometimes untidy.

but Jezebel was always super dooper neat.

Jezebel always kept her room tidy, and she always put her things back in their boxes . . .

and she cleaned up after the cat.

When she went out to play with her friends,

Jezebel always kept clean. (She still liked to have two baths every day.)

She always wrote her "thank you" letters, in neat
writing, without being reminded,

and at school, she was best at everything.

When she had spots, she always took her medicine
(and said, "Thank you.")

She could do up buttons, and tie real bows on her lace-ups.

Jezebel always ate up her meals. She always put
her knife and fork together,

and she *never* picked her nose.

Jezebel told other children not to do things . . .

because it was nice being perfect.

When the Prime Minister heard about Jezebel,
she sent her a special medal for being good,

and a special statue of Jezebel was put up in the park, to remind everybody else to try to be perfect.

She even went on television, in a special show
to talk about herself and her medal,

and the cups she had won for being polite, being
spotless, being helpful, being best at sums, reading,
poetry and writing.

At school, Super Dooper Jezebel wouldn't do *anything* wrong . . .

like the other noisy children who weren't perfect . . .

CLUMP!